THE ANGEL TREE

by Helena Clare Pittman
pictures by Jo Ellen McAllister Stammen

Dial Books for Young Readers
New York

Published by Dial Books for Young Readers
A member of Penguin Putnam Inc.
375 Hudson Street
New York, New York 10014

Text copyright © 1998 by Helena Clare Pittman
Pictures copyright © 1998 by Jo Ellen McAllister Stammen
All rights reserved
Designed by Julie Rauer
Printed in Hong Kong on acid-free paper
First Edition
1 3 5 7 9 10 8 6 4 2

Library of Congress Cataloging in Publication Data
Pittman, Helena Clare.
The angel tree/by Helena Clare Pittman: pictures by
Jo Ellen McAllister Stammen.—1st ed.
p. cm.
Summary: When his special friend Cyrus McCafferty, aging benefactor to
Bordenville's children, moves away, Jake celebrates their friendship by buying the
giant spruce usually reserved for Cyrus, and a Christmas miracle occurs.
ISBN 0-8037-1939-6 (trade).—ISBN 0-8037-1941-8 (lib. bdg.)
[1. Christmas trees—Fiction. 2. Christmas—Fiction.
3. Friendship—Fiction.] I. McAllister Stammen, Jo Ellen, ill. II. Title.
PZ7.P689An 1998 [Fic]—dc21 97-26667 CIP AC

The art was prepared using dry pastels on dark gray pastel paper.

For my sister Jolene—forever

—H.C.P.

To the source of all our good deeds

—J.M.S.

Old man Cyrus McCafferty lived at the top of High Street. He had lived alone, except for his cook and servants, as long as anyone could remember. He was so kindly that people often said the angels themselves must have kept him company. He treated everyone in town, especially the children, as if they were his own family. When he passed our front yard on his way home after buying the newspaper, he always called out to me: "How are you, Jake? Mighty fine day, isn't it?"

"Sure is, Mr. McCafferty!" I'd call back.

But like my father and me, who had only each other, Mr. McCafferty had just one sister, and she lived in Indiana. Maybe Bordenville's children were like the grandchildren he never had. Maybe that's why on the Friday after Thanksgiving his cook always opened the front door to us all so we could decorate the huge Christmas spruce that stood in the big hall.

The servants brought trays of cakes, and boxes of ornaments covered the floor. We hung the branches with bright decorations until the cakes were gone and the boxes were empty, and the big boughs sagged with ornaments that had been in the McCafferty family for generations.

So began the magic that lasted until Christmas night. The hall rang with our happy voices while the old man sat in his armchair, tapping his cane and calling out our names.

One of the ornaments was a crystal globe that held a tiny Christmas tree. It was filled with water and drifting flakes that looked like snow when you shook it. I think Mr. McCafferty knew it was my favorite. "Beautiful, isn't it, Jake?" he once asked. "It was given to me when I was your age."

The servants, who were as kind as Mr. McCafferty, smiled at our merriment. "Little angels!" I heard the cook say once, and I never forgot that. I guess because of what people said about the angels keeping old Mr. McCafferty company.

When the tree was finished, we all hailed, "Merry Christmas, Mr. McCafferty!" Then the cook led us to the dining room and a basket of wrapped ornaments, one for each of us, to hang on our own trees.

At the other end of High Street, where our house stood and the corner turned into Broadway, there was an empty lot where Christmas trees were sold. I could watch from my bedroom window as people came to buy their trees. The big perfect Norway spruce was always the first to leave the lot, driven in the gardener's truck up the hill to the great old house.

It was part of Christmas to watch the man in the lot pulling out trees and tying them to the tops of cars. Tall ones, short ones, delicate and full—the trees left to cheer houses and light windows. Finally only those that were lopsided or too skinny remained.

And every year it wasn't until late Christmas Eve that my father and I walked to the corner to buy one of the last trees. The man always accepted whatever my father could pay—five dollars, seven dollars, maybe three dollars, which was sometimes all he had.

"It's been a lean year," my father would say quietly to the man.

"Next Christmas will be better," he'd say to me as we walked home. Sometimes on that walk my father would talk about a Christmas when my mother was alive and I was very small. He spoke softly as I struggled to remember the woman who looked like me in the photograph on my father's dresser.

Just as Mr. McCafferty's tree was always the first, ours must surely have been the last. Yet bringing it back near midnight with my father was as much a part of the magic of Christmas as Mr. McCafferty's tree.

So it was a shock to realize that things had changed the year the windows went dark in the house on High Street's hill.

One by one the trees in the lot were sold, but the perfect Norway spruce remained. That's how everyone knew for certain that Mr. McCafferty was gone. Grown-ups whispered that something must have happened. After all, Mr. McCafferty was old.

One afternoon I walked up the hill to look into the big front windows. The hall was dark. The dining room was empty. I could almost imagine the basket of wrapped ornaments on the table, could almost see the cook's kind face.

"Hey, Jake!" someone called. I turned, half expecting to see Mr. McCafferty, but it was Mr. Barnes, the mailman.

"Where's Mr. McCafferty?" I asked, afraid to hear the answer.

"He's moved to his sister's in Indiana," said Mr. Barnes.

"Oh!" I said with relief.

Mr. Barnes hesitated. "I guess you could write him a note on one of these envelopes. They're going to his new address." He gave me a pen.

I didn't need to think long about what I wanted to say. "Thanks for everything, Mr. McCafferty. Bordenville will miss you. Jake."

That Christmas Eve my father and I set out for our tree. The
Norway spruce stood in the empty lot looking strange in a corner by
itself. The man was ready to close. He was wrapped in a scarf, and his
cheeks glowed pink from the nipping cold. Our breath hung in the air,
lit by the street lamp as my father examined the scrawny trees which
were left.

"How about that one?" I asked suddenly, pointing to the spruce.

My father laughed in surprise. "It won't fit through the door."

"It's yours for five dollars," said the man.

My father looked at me. Then he looked over at that lonely tree, naked except for a sprinkling of the snow which had begun to fall. "I guess we could cut the trunk."

He reached into his pocket, pulled out a folded five-dollar bill, and gave it to the man.

We staggered home under the load. After we set down the tree at
our front door, my father just stood there shaking his head. "We'll
have to leave it out here until morning. It will take too long to cut that
trunk."

"Until morning?" I repeated with disappointment.

My father hugged me. "We'll get up early, Jake." he said.

I went upstairs, but couldn't sleep. It was strange to think of putting
up the tree on Christmas morning. Strange, too, that Mr. McCafferty's
tree stood in our front yard.

Then something happened that I wonder at still. A soft melody, one I'd never heard, floated up to my room. I rose and looked outside. The snow had almost stopped. Standing in the middle of the yard, its branches opened to the cold, starry Christmas sky, was the spruce. A circle of carolers surrounded the tree. Bathed in the light of a fat Christmas moon, they danced and sang their beautiful carol, hanging delicate crystal decorations and icy garlands on the boughs of Mr. McCafferty's tree.

I tiptoed downstairs and opened the front door. It creaked on its hinges and one of the carolers turned toward me.

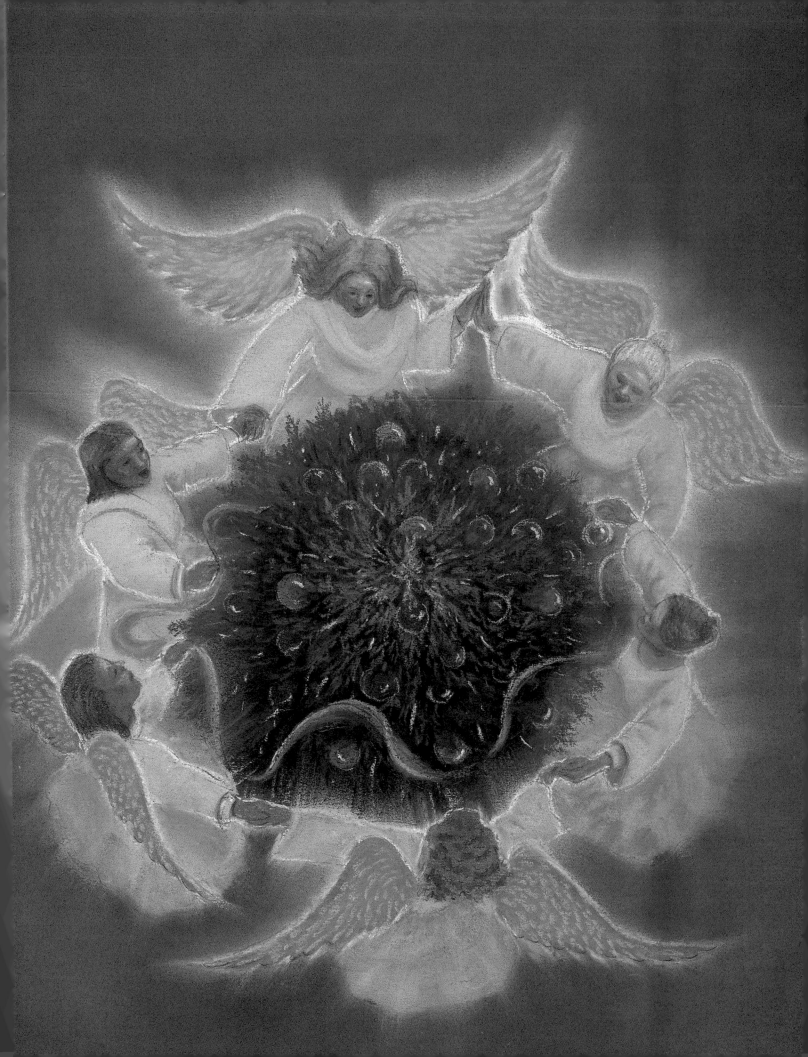

"Would you like one?" she asked, pointing to the ornaments.

Then I remembered what people had always said about the angels and Mr. McCafferty. "It's true," I whispered.

The angel smiled and I recognized Mr. McCafferty's old cook. She lifted a crystal globe from its branch and held it out to me. Inside was a tiny Christmas tree and drifting flakes that looked like snow.

She pointed to another of the carolers, whose smile was familiar. It was the woman who looked like me in the photograph on my father's dresser.

Then, with their beautiful song, the merry carolers faded and were gone. The tree stood alone in the front yard, its boughs covered in crystal decorations. I gazed at it until my eyelids drooped.

Back in my room I put the crystal globe on the table next to my bed. In the morning when I woke to the sound of my father's saw, it was the first thing I looked for. But only a puddle of water reflected the light from the window.

Downstairs the Christmas tree filled half the living room. My father was struggling to stand it up. "Give me a hand, will you, Jake?" he asked.

After we settled it into the stand, we stood back to admire it. The tree touched the ceiling, and the aroma of pine filled the house.

"Were there any ornaments on it?" I asked.

"Ornaments?" my father repeated, and shook his head.

I opened the front door. The pine log my father had sawn from the tree was sitting in the snow. On the step was a package wrapped in brown paper, postmarked "Indiana." I picked it up and opened it. The note read, "Thanks, Jake. I didn't want to miss a year, and thought you'd like to have this. Merry Christmas. Cyrus McCafferty."

Wrapped in a piece of Christmas paper was the crystal globe.

It took all the lights we had to cover the spruce. The crystal globe sparkled, turning on its wire. "Sure is a beauty." my father said when the tree was finished. Then he added softly. "I wish your mother could see it."

I just smiled. And while it had been what my father called a lean year, he'd managed to pile the blanket on the floor with presents.

There was a package on our steps every Christmas for the next few years. though I never saw those carolers again. But until this day. at Christmastime I watch the crystal globe turning on its wire. and I remember that night on the front lawn. "Merry Christmas. Mr. McCafferty." I always whisper.